P9-ARH-768

"I'm only 3 years old, dad. I'm just a little boy, your boy, your son. Please dad, why did you abandon us?"

At that moment I woke up crying, my whole body shaking. I couldn't stop my heart from pounding. I didn't want to wake Laura, who have fallen asleep watching television in the room below. I got out of bed and walked slowly to the bathroom. I closed the door, shut off the night light and let my fear fill the room along with the darkness.

The story in this book is the product of my imagination, although based on some facts from my own life experience as a child. Names, characters, places and incidents are fictitious. Any resemblance with real life events and names is purely coincidental.

SPECIAL DEDICATION

I never realized that writing this book would be so intensive, deeply challenging, and at times, very emotional.

To God, for giving life and the road I had to walk to get to where I am today. It was hard at times but it was worth it.

To my wonderful mother, whose infinite love helped to shape who I am today. Words can't express the gratitude I feel toward you. I love you mama.

To Dave, thank you for the patience you have shown during our past 14 years together. I know it has not been easy for you to learn and to understand many aspects of my culture, language and beliefs.

What really amazes me the most is how you took the time to teach me about American culture without taking away my own; for that I will always love you.

A special thanks to Deb Rozak and Brad Lisak for taking time way from their busy schedule to help me edit this book. You both did an amazing job and for that I'm very thankful.

I want to extend a special dedication to Lucinda, a woman who has been my inspiration. She pushed my boundaries and she taught me to believe in myself with her words of wisdom. God bless every one of you.

PROLOGUE

"*Suddenly, I come to the realization that my mother is no longer the skinny, young woman I remember as a child. These days, her skin is wrinkled and the struggles of her life are starting to show in her face. Nevertheless, she continues to be the leader of the herd*"

From Ashes to Dreams... My life, my story

Spring is almost here. The temperature outside starts to feel warm, the flowers are blooming in the garden and the aroma of my mother's roses is intoxicating to my soul. Inside my mother's house, everyone has gathered in the living room. But it is a sad time, full of uncertainties. We have no idea what's going to become of our family. Our mother is gravely ill.

Everything started last week. I traveled to Houston, Texas to attend a seminar for an upcoming photography exhibit featuring ten prominent photographers who were scheduled to display their work in a major art show. I remember waking up that morning unease. I looked outside my hotel room, there weren't any clouds in the sky and visibility was great across the valley. I looked at the clock on the nightstand and I realized I was running late. I took a quick shower and dressed up before making myself a cup of coffee. "God, how much I miss the coffee my mother used to make us as a kids. This is crap and it doesn't even come close to hers.

As I finished drinking the coffee, there was a knock on the door. It was Richard, one of my colleagues.

"Come on Antonio, we are running late and we still have to find our way around this city" he said with a look of worry in his face.

"Relax Richard, I took care of everything. I made reservations last night for a limousine to come pick us up. Do you think I'm brave enough to venture in a big city like this?" Richard looked at me in disbelieve. He shook his head and went back to his room to pick up his jacket and backpack. Right outside the hotel lobby there was a white limousine waiting for us.

"You do like to travel in style, don't you" Richard commented with a playful smile.

"There's a lot of things I like to do in style, I deserve it" I replied back to him while handling the directions to the driver.

We spent most of the morning listening to speeches, watching videos and doing teleconferences with people in London and Germany.

At noon time we went to the restaurant that was located at the conference center. We were having lunch with some of our colleagues and talking about the event that took place during the morning when my phone rang. I wasn't sure why, but a sense of fear came over me and by the time I answered the phone, I already knew what the person on the other end of the line was going to tell me.

It was my sister Delia. She sounded as if she had been crying. "Antonio, you need to come home right away. Our mother is not doing well and the doctor doesn't think she's going to hold on much longer."

For the past two months my mother's health had been deteriorating and she had started to forget names and things. It had gotten difficult for her to take long walks and her appetite had declined to the point that her doctor had strongly recommended a feeding tube. She had refused. My mother was 76 years old and had lived a full life. She believed that her fate was in God's hands and my siblings and I had reluctantly agreed to respect her wishes in the matter. She believed that if it were time to go home, no one should stand in the way.

"What's going on Antonio? You are shaking and your face just turns white as a ghost" Richard asked.

"It's my mother. Look, I need to leave, she's dying. Could you please excuse me from the conference and take some notes for me?"

"Are you going to be alright? I can go back with you if you want. Remember, there's another conference coming up in few month"

No, I'll be fine but thanks". I patted Richard on his shoulder, excused myself from the table and left the restaurant.

On my way to the hotel, I called my secretary and booked the first flight to

Boston that afternoon. By the time I touched down at the Logan Airport, my brother Felipe and my son Fernando were already waiting for me at the gate. There was no luggage to pick up because I always travel light. Fernando was happy to see me despite the sad circumstances. Felipe explained what had happened to mom the previous day so that I knew what to expect when we arrived home. The day I had left for my trip, I had visited my mother to say good-bye. Although fragile, she had been stable enough to sit down in her recliner. I wasn't sure if she had understood most of our conversation but she hadn't seemed to care. The family had decided that my mother, even at her age, would never be placed in a nursing home.

Instead we had all agreed to take turns staying the night in her house to look after her. My siblings had understood the fact that my work required me to be away for days or weeks at a time, but whenever I had free time I would bring my son and stay for the weekend so that everyone could do their things. On the night of my departure my mother had started vomiting and having seizures. The nurse had come to the house that night and, after doing some tests, had called the doctor. He concluded that our mother had had another heart attack. "There is nothing I can do except to try and keep her comfortable," he told my siblings, and recommended that they gather the family because she was not going to live long.

CHAPTER I

The waiting

"Mama, how did everything begin? How did we manage to survive those years?"

Tears were streaming down my cheeks despite my best efforts to hide the pain in my face. My mama, achingly fragile, was lying there in her bed. At 76 years old she still looked amazing for someone who had spent her entire life struggling to keep her family together. The scars of a rough life showed in her face: scars of a life filled with uncertainty, pain and poverty.

"We had a good life," she said, in a now-too-rare moment of clarity. "It was rough and we didn't have many material things but we had each other and that, my son, is what made our family so rich. Nobody can take that away."

I sat in silence for a few minutes. The room became still. There weren't any words I could say that would describe the emotions I was feeling.

"I'm sorry," mama said with tears in her eyes.

From Ashes to Dreams… My life, my story
"Why are you sorry, mama?"

She tried to sit up in bed but became
short of breath. "I'm sorry for keeping
your father's memory to myself, but I
never had the courage to speak about him.
Even today, on my deathbed, I find it hard
to think of him. I didn't want you kids to
be hurt. I only wanted to protect you."

I took my mother's hand and placed it on
my cheek. "Mama please, there's nothing to
be sorry for. You did what you thought was
best for us under those circumstances and
besides, look at us now. You did a fine
job raising us on your own. You have all
your grand-children who think the world of
you, including Fernando who isn't your own
blood. From the moment he first came to
this house you treated him the same as you
did the other kids. You proved to Grandma
Estella that a human being always has
enough love to give others if they truly
want to share. We have the utmost respect
for you mama. You were everything to us:
mother, father and best friend. You
protected us the way a lioness protects

its cubs."

Mama seemed lost in her memories.

She didn't say anything, but just lay there staring at the ceiling fan.

"Do you remember Delia's wedding?" I asked, hoping to drag her out of her reverie and keep her here with me in the present. "I asked you to dance and you were nervous because as a teenager you never went to a dance - but once you hit the floor you were glowing. It's hard to believe it was only a year ago! Do you remember dancing with me? The song was perfect; 'The Dance'. I'll never forget that moment, mama."

Mom looked at me and smiled vaguely. Heartsick, I wasn't sure if she understood what I was saying or if her mind had betrayed her again and had temporarily robbed her of her memories of the wedding.

"We all love you mom." As I said this I lowered myself down and kissed her forehead. "Now try and get some sleep, alright?"

She sank into a dream again. I stood there in the dark watching my mother sleeping peacefully, my mind wondering back into our past.

I can't help thinking how many sleepless nights she spent worrying about her children and how to make ends meet. How lucky we were to have this amazing woman for our mother, but how painful it was to watch her slipping away. If you only knew dad what an amazing woman she is. I shake the thoughts out of my head realizing that nothing else matters anymore; our past is our past and right now, I have to focus my attention on her until God decides to take her home.

I left the room for a moment. The only light in the room came from a candle that we kept near a statue of our Lady of Guadalupe, my mother's patron saint. Mama was very devoted to her.

I walked into the living room where my wife and family were gathered, having coffee and watching television. My nieces and nephews have no real idea of what we went through so that they could have a chance at a better life.

"How's she doing?" my brother Felipe asked.

"She's doing fine right now. She's resting peacefully. Her doctor gave her some medication and it appears to be doing a good job. She has such a strong will to live! I don't know how she manages to take a breath."

My sister, overhearing our comments, smiled ruefully, as if acknowledging the fact that our mother's time was nearing its end. She walked toward the window and although she was looking at the garden, her gaze seemed to be focused somewhere else. She spoke in a voice thick with emotion.

"It's been such a long journey for mom. She struggled all those years to keep the family together and now here we are trying to keep her comfortable. It seems so little compared with what she did for us in her life!"

After she spoke, Delia broke down and started to cry. I took her in my arms and she wept quietly into my chest. We all fell silent for a moment, the only sound coming from the television set tuned to the big game in an attempt to keep ourselves distracted and to keep the sadness at bay.

Watching us from the other side of the room was my wife Laura. Seeing my sister crying, she approaches us and took her by the hand.

"Delia, you need to be strong right now, I know it's not easy but right now, your mother needs you with her. I'm going to the kitchen to make you some Chamomile tea that will help you"

"Thank you Laura. My mother always spoke so highly of you. She loves you very much. You always were there for her, not like a daughter in law but like a true daughter. I'm so glad Antonio married you." Delia gave Laura a hug and both women left the room leaving me alone with my thoughts.

CHAPTER II

Fernando

Our son Fernando was deeply affected by my mother's condition. Before I arrived he had not left my mother's bedside. He spoke to her the way he always did when she took care of him while Laura and I spent long hours at work so we could provide him with a good home and education. Laura and I had been married for 15 years now. Laura loves our culture. She is part French and part Irish, but has always found Hispanics and Hispanic culture alluring, even during her teenage years telling her friends she wanted to marry a Hispanic man.

On our first anniversary we went to see her doctor to find out why she couldn't get pregnant. After several tests the results came back.

"Good morning," Dr. Kelly greeted us as we entered his office.

"Well, Dr. Kelly, do you have any news for us?" I asked impatiently.

"All the results came back. Laura, I'm afraid to tell you that your ovaries are not producing eggs strong enough to be fertilized. There are several procedures that we could try but they're very expensive and insurance won't cover them because they're still in trial stages. To be honest, the chances of them helping are slim. I'm sorry. I wish I had better news for you."

Laura burst into tears but quickly recovered her composure. "Dr. Kelly, I think it's a good idea if my husband and I go home and talk about our options before making any other decisions," Laura said sadly.

Laura fell into a depression for the next few weeks. I thought it would be best to give her some space so she could think and grieve. Then one morning I was sitting at the table having my breakfast when she came bouncing down the stairs singing, with a bright smile on her face.

"What's gotten into you?" I asked happily but with a look of confusion.

"Antonio, I had a dream last night. I dreamt that someone left a baby boy on our doorstep with a note attached to his shirt. The note read: 'I know how much you want to have a son. I am too young to care for my baby and I believe that you and your husband can give him a good home and love him as much as I would.'

"I think this dream was a sign. Here we are trying to have a baby of our own when there are so many children out there in need of a good home and family. Maybe our destiny is to adopt one of those kids."

"Laura, did Dr. Kelly put you on any type of medication? Because I love the idea but I want to make sure it's not a weird reaction to her medication, and that you're serious about this," I joked.

Laura laughed and for the first time since we had left Dr. Kelly's office, I noticed a bright glowing aura around her. I knew she was serious about the possibility of adoption and I was awfully excited about it myself.

We called Dr. Kelly and he recommended a good adoption agency. Within six months we had all the paperwork filled out and had undergone all the testing needed prior to the adoption.

Another long year passed before we were matched with a child. On the day of our appointment with the adoption agency we were both nervous and anxious at the same time. On our way to the agency Laura was lost in thought. "What are you thinking?" I asked.

"Antonio, what if this is a mistake? What if we turn out to be bad parents?"

Without waiting for an answer she turned her head toward the window and lost herself in thought once again, wrestling in silence with her doubts and her fears.

"You must be Antonio and Laura Colon," the receptionist remarked when we arrived.

"Yes ma'am, we are. We are here to meet with Mrs. Anderson."

"Have a seat. She'll be with you shortly." She paged the social worker and returned to her work.

Laura turned toward me and taking my hand, she smiled. "Honey, here we are, minutes away from becoming parents: no waiting, no prenatal screening and best of all, no labor pains!" We started to giggle but our giddiness quickly dissipated when we heard the door open and Mrs. Anderson called us to her office.

"Please sit," Mrs. Anderson said, gesturing at the two chairs across from her desk.

"First of all, I want to give you this note," she said, handing a sheet of paper to us. "Fernando's mother left him at one of the local churches. Nobody knows who she is or her whereabouts." This, she indicated in the note we now held, "had been attached to the blanket. It tells of his Hispanic heritage and explains that she was too young to take care of her child and that her family didn't approve of her pregnancy.

"Now it's time for you to meet your prospective son. Are you ready or would you like a moment?"

"Please, we want to meet him right away! We can't wait!"

She picked up her phone and asked that Fernando be brought to her office.

When Fernando entered the office he had a look of combined hope and despair on his little face. He came running to me and hugged my leg as if pleading, "Please don't leave me here alone!" We fell completely in love with him in an instant. He was only three years old: the same age I had been when

I lost my father.

Mrs. Anderson watched for a while then offered to leave us alone with him for a brief visit. "When I come back we'll discuss the steps necessary to finalize the adoption."

Fernando was enchanting. When Mrs. Anderson returned and Fernando reluctantly allowed himself to be escorted from the room, Laura and I immediately informed her of our decision to accept the referral. "Well then," she smiled, "you may take him home with you when you leave today. We'll monitor your family for the next six months or so, and if all goes well we'll make a recommendation to the courts that the adoption be finalized. If the court agrees, you'll become Fernando's legal parents."

Laura and I took some time off from work so that Fernando could get used to his new environment and his new parents. We took him to the parks, we bought him new clothing and toys, and we learned to love him as our own.

When the time came for Laura and I to return to work, we had to rely on my mother to baby-sit because of our demanding work schedules. My mother fell in love with Fernando from the beginning. The feeling was mutual: he loved his grandma so much that he often cried, pleading to spend the night over her house.

Tearing myself from these wonderful memories, I decided to step outside onto the porch to collect my thoughts and get some fresh air. The air felt clean and pure. It was the beginning of May and the scent of flowers from Mama's garden perfumed the air. The garden was blooming with an impressive variety of roses and carnations. This garden was my mother's pride and joy and every year she made sure we planted more flowers.

My memory was pulled further back by the scent of flowers, to the spring days of my earliest childhood before the loss of my father: the flowers in the garden, the aroma of my mother's roses, and all of us playing outside in the sun...

I heard the screen door open behind me and I looked back to see Fernando standing there.

"Hi buddy, how are you holding up?" I asked.

"I'm alright dad, just a little tired. But it's been a tough day for all of us."

"I know, but right now grandma needs us. We have to stay strong."

Fernando walked past me and stood at the railing looking toward the garden, his back toward me.

"Dad, how come nobody talks about grandpa? What happened to him? It's almost as if he never existed. I thought that maybe everyone was holding out on me because I'm adopted, but even my cousins don't seem to know much about him."

"It's a long story son. And don't for one second think that you're less a part of this family because you were adopted. You've been a part of this family from the moment we brought you home and you have the right to know everything there is to know about us."

"And what's up with you, dad? Ever since I came to live with you I feel as if you're holding onto something very deep. Sometimes I hear you talking in your sleep about stuff that means nothing to me. You occasionally cry out. I jump out of bed and run to your room only to find you sleeping peacefully again. I asked mom what was going on but she told me that I should ask you. I decided to wait for the right moment."

"What makes you think that this is right time?"

"I'm not sure… perhaps because grandma isn't doing well and I think her time is now and I want to know what she went through before she dies."

I stood there for a moment taking everything in; wondering what would be the best way to tell Fernando the story of our life. Shortly before I had asked her to marry me I had told Laura about my past. I had known deep inside my heart that she was the one for me and she had deserved the whole truth about me before deciding to share the rest of her life with me. But how would I explain it to a fifteen year old boy, my son, without altering his perceptions of me? This was not going to be easy for him and it was definitely not going to be easy for me. There was so much pain; so many partially buried memories that now had to be unearthed once again. How could I let myself remember the things that I had tried for so long to forget?

"Let's sit down son, this could take a while. I've been afraid to tell you this, afraid that you'll think less me for it. But I'm also afraid to open up this part of my life that I thought I had let go some years ago. I hope that by the time I'm finished you'll be able to understand everything."

"Tell me how it all started," Fernando prompted.

"I've always thought of people as birds and life as the wind. Depending on the current you can fly as high as you wish. But if there is no wind to support your wings then you have to fly low or fall from the sky.

"It all started after I met your mother: the nightmares, the depression and anxiety. I couldn't handle it. It was smothering our relationship. That's when I decided to write a letter to my father. I needed to let go of that painful past and that was the best way I knew how to do it."

"My story starts when I was in my late 20's and I was accomplishing many things. Critics were reviewing my work and I was traveling all over the country. Laura and I had started dating. I knew she was the one for me from the moment we met. After several months, we discussed marriage and raising a family. I wanted to be upfront with her about my past. I didn't want any secrets in our relationship so one day I sat with her at dinner and I told her my story. She was gracious and understanding and completely unfazed. We dated for a year and a half before we got married. Right after our wedding we moved in together. We both wanted kids and tried from the very beginning to conceive. Then one night I started having these horrible nightmares...

Chapter III

The dreams

"I'm only 3 years old, dad. I'm just a little boy, your boy, your son. Please dad, why did you abandon us?"

At that moment I woke up crying, my whole body shaking. I couldn't stop my heart from pounding. I didn't want to wake Laura, who fell asleep watching television in the room below. I got out of bed and walked slowly to the bathroom. I closed the door, shut off the night light and let my fear fill the room along with the darkness. For a long time I just stood there covered in a cold sweat, trying to shake off what had just happened to me. I kept telling myself that it was just a dream, or more accurately a nightmare, just a figment of my imagination. But deep inside my heart I knew that my past was catching up to me. I let the water run in the sink until it was ice cold and splashed it all over my face, trying to cool both my flushed face and my fevered mind.

I returned to my bedroom, lay on my cramped back, and stared at the ceiling fan. I tried to relax and fall back to sleep but the embers of my panic flared up each time I closed my eyes and I spent the rest of the night awake in my torment.

The following morning I got up and sat at the table drinking coffee. Laura eventually awoke and came into the kitchen. She greeted me happily and began to prepare her breakfast; talking about the shows she had watched on television the previous evening and her plans for the day ahead. But my responses must not have been as cheerful as I had tried to make them. Her pleasant chatter grew more tentative and she darted concerned glances at me. At last, she abruptly turned to me and asked what was happening. "You look as if you haven't slept in weeks... Are you still having those nightmares?" she asked.

"Yeah, last night was one of the worst I've had in a long time. I got up, went in the bathroom, and splashed cold water on my face to try to release some of the tension but when I tried to get back to sleep I just couldn't close my eyes. I was afraid. I wanted to tell you but you were sound asleep and I didn't want to wake you."

"Do you know that you often talk and cry out in your sleep? But you speak in Spanish so I don't know exactly what's haunting you."

"They're all about my childhood and are so vivid. Last night I was dreaming that I was back in Puerto Rico and I tried to get on the plane to come home but the plane took off without me. I ran and ran but it was impossible to reach it. I went to see when the next plane was leaving for the States only to be told that there wasn't one for another six months. That's when I ran back to the runway and started running and screaming for the plane to stop. It was horrible. The thought of being trapped was unbearable," I shuddered.

It was actually an amazing feat that I could speak Spanish in my sleep. All the years with English as my primary language and a desire to leave my past in Puerto Rico behind had made it difficult for me to express myself in my once-native Spanish. Apparently though, I could switch back to Spanish in my sleep.

The nightmares continued for weeks. One evening during the opening of one of my photography exhibits, a stranger introduced himself to me. He was handsome, about 40 years old, and well-dressed. He started complimenting my artwork and asking me simple questions about my life. But as the questions started to get personal, I grew uncomfortable. A group of people had gathered around us and they too began asking questions and it suddenly seemed too much. Reflexively, defensively, and to my shame, I once again began to lie about who I really was - not because I was ashamed of my past but because I was afraid that Americans, with all that they have, would look at me with pity if they knew my story. I didn't want anyone's pity. My defense mechanism had been to try to convince myself that I was someone else. I had been living a lie for too many years, pretending to be someone who I wasn't and had never been, and now had to face the fear of being exposed as a liar.

I did not grow up in a middle class family nor did I come from the city of Ponce as I had often told people. I did not go to a Catholic school or wear the latest fashions. The people around me, including those whom I had known for years, didn't know anything true about my past. Everything they knew came from that little boy I once was who dreamt of becoming the man I am today. A boy who came from nothing to the land of opportunity where he wanted to forge a new life. A proud boy who wanted to make his own way, reliant on no one, perceived as an equal. At that point of my life I was also living in the public eye. I was an established photographer. People were starting to recognize me everywhere I went. I wasn't sure how the public would react. What would they think of me if the truth got out? Would they still like me? I had kept my private life behind this dark curtain for so long, the curtain had come to separate me from the rest of the world.

The nightmares, followed so closely by my acknowledgment that I was a stranger in my own life, left me mentally exhausted. I knew that the nightmares sprung from my deceit. My past was haunting me and I had to confront it, to expose it, in order to heal my fractured self and vanquish my demons.

I went home on the evening of May 15, 1995 and sat at my desk intent on telling my story, trying to figure out how best to begin. How could I explain to my friends, my fans, what I had endured and why I had felt the need to hide it from them? How to place it all into words for the world to read? I had never attempted to communicate anything so personal and so powerful.

Then it struck me: this wasn't just about the deceit in my professional and personal life. No, my marriage and the prospect of having children had triggered these nightmares. I was terrified of turning into my father.

I decided to go directly to the heart of the matter - to write about my past from the moment my father died. Why not tell the world that behind this man with a promising future and career there was the dark and horrible life of a poverty-stricken family with six children - among them, this boy, now a man, who now would dare to break his family silence? Why not tell the world of a boy who dreamed of rising from the ashes of a broken and penniless family to become the success he always dreamed he would be?

My father was the source of our family pain. He was the ghost behind my nightmares. I held him responsible for our suffering. To vent my anger at him I would write him a letter explaining how I feel about him even though he's been dead and gone for so very long.

This wasn't going to be easy. I needed to be true to myself and to others. I had come to this country to become someone, to escape my past, and yet this ghost of my past continues to haunt me and wouldn't let me go until I let it go. I also needed to take in consideration the fact that

From Ashes to Dreams... My life, my story

although this is my story, it also involves others who like me had to endure the same fate as I did and I needed to make sure that this letter wouldn't hurt anyone. Fernando, this is my story, a story about a boy with high hopes, a boy who dared to dream big and a boy willing to fight his past so that he could have a brighter future not just for himself but also for his family. Son, this is my story...

"As I sat down at my desk and started writing this letter, I never thought that my feelings were going to play a trick on me. Suddenly, as if a door opened wide, all my childhood memories started to manifest right in front of my eyes"

CHARTER IV

The letter

May 15, 1995

Dear Father,

I know it sounds weird that I'm writing this letter to you since you've been dead for over 25 years. I feel the need to write this letter to let you know the way my life has been warped because of your wrong choices. You are the source of my shame and fear, and I suffer for your sins.

Dad, I'm about to become a father myself and I don't know if I'm really prepared to become one. I never had a father to show me how. I want to be a good provider not just for my son but for my wife as well. I want my son to be proud of me.

The thought of writing about my past has crossed my mind several times in the past but because of family sensitivities, I was afraid of hurting the ones I love the most. I tried to push the idea away but nightmares about that time have torn at my peace of mind. Many nights I have lain in bed with a pillow over my head so nobody

could hear me cry. I hate those
nightmares, dad. I need them to go away
forever. The pain in my soul has grown
stronger than the fear of telling our
story. I hope that in doing so I can
finally expose the dark heart of my dreams
to the light and banish them for good.

I can't speak about you as a person
because I never had the chance to really
get to know you. I never learned anything
about the man who gave me life. To this
day nobody in the family mentions your
name nor speaks about you because you
brought so much shame and pain into our
lives.

Since my marriage I have suffered from
these nightmares about that horrible past
I cannot seem to shake. Because of you,
dad, I lived a life of poverty, of begging
neighbors and strangers for money to help
my mother buy food for the table. Alone, I
could have suffered in silence, but my
demons are cutting me off from those
around me. Forgive me, father, for what
I'm about to tell you but I feel that it's

necessary for the sanity and health of my soul, and for all those I touch.

In case you have forgotten which one of your children I am, let me refresh your memory: I was born March 6, 1965, the fourth child, remember? We were such a happy family. One year after my birth my sister was born and two years later, my youngest brother. Now there were six of us children in what people called the happiest family in the neighborhood. People were so wrong. All the time you professed love for us you were living a double life with a mistress, who by the way was also married. My mother was naïve: too trusting and too busy raising your children at home while you were off having your affair.

Then one afternoon the police showed up at our house to deliver the bad news. The woman with whom you had pursued your secret affair for years had shot and killed you in her house. She never went to jail because in her statement in court she told the judge that you attacked her.

Dad, I was just 3 years old, just a little boy. I can still close my eyes and hear my mother screaming and crying when my neighbors gave her the news. At that time I had no clue what was happening around me. There was a big commotion. Everyone was running in and out of our two- bedroom rundown home.

Some cried and some whispered among themselves. Nobody spoke aloud and even if someone did, I couldn't hear a thing because my poor mother would not stop crying. All I remember is sitting in a corner and watching this tragic moment unfolded before my eyes. You were not the only thing that died that day. No, besides losing our father, though we didn't know it then, we also lost our best chance for a better future. You shattered our lives.

There were whispered rumors that your family was aware of this affair yet kept it a secret from my mother. I like to believe that if they had said something to mom, perhaps she could have done something and you would still be alive today and we would never have suffered what was to come. And although Mom never did learn the true motive behind your death, she suspected it had to do with money. Right after your death my mother found a bundle of cancelled checks in a locked box, checks made out to your mistress. When my mother went to the bank to withdraw money for us, the bank teller told her that the account was almost empty. Dad, we had been considered middle class and my mother knew there should have been money in that account. What happened to it?

Because I was only three years old, I couldn't comprehend what was happening to us but as I got older, I started to understand what your poor judgment had done to our family and I became angry and embittered. I believe that you spent all our savings on your mistress and I can't comprehend how you could have done that when you had six little children to feed. Some people believe that she was blackmailing you for a child she had with you. If that was the case, you weren't man enough to confront the situation with dignity. I know that our mother would have understood. Because of your selfishness and cowardice, you lost your life and our family's savings, and in doing so stole our childhood.

The years that followed your death were marked by struggle, loneliness and uncertainty. Nothing was ever going to be the same. You left a mother with six kids, all under the age of eleven, with no money but an inadequate monthly social security allowance to fend for themselves. Mama didn't know what to do; she wasn't prepared to take on the task of raising her children alone. She was accustomed to staying home and caring for us because you were the provider.

My poor mother never had the chance to grieve your death because she was too busy trying to figure out where our next meals were going to come from and making sure that her children grew up to be good citizens with a proper education. Many times during the night I heard my mother praying alone in her bedroom, asking God for help and strength so that she could be a good mother. I won't lie to you and say that she never cried. She cried in bed, in the bathroom, and at the kitchen table. You have no idea how hard it was for a child to see his mother in so much pain. Some nights when I heard mom cry I wanted to get up and assure her that everything was going to be alright. However, I couldn't even convince myself of that so I closed my eyes and went to sleep. At times our lives seemed about to crumble from under our feet.

I have been told that at the time you married my mother, your mother, my Grandma Estella, disapproved because she had had higher expectations for you. Your family was considered to be upper-class while my mother's families were all farmers with little or no money. Your death did not improve her attitude toward us. It grew worse, with her treating us like outcasts. There was never enough time for us. I wish I could remember my grandmother giving me a kiss or holding me in her lap telling me a children's story. I wish I could recall hearing her say even once that she loved me.

Do you know our grandmother over 15 years to step inside of our house even though she lived next door to us? I truly believe that grandma blamed my mother for what happened to you.

There were times when I walked past her house and she wouldn't acknowledge that I was there. Even worse, sometimes I would go in for a visit, sit around in the living room, and then leave because she wouldn't come out of her bedroom. Her behavior left a scar in my heart.

She never had the affection toward us that she had with our cousins. Your sister, whose husband died months after you in a tragic accident, got all the help she needed from grandma even though her husband had left his family with a good pension to live on: something you had failed to do.

Ironically, when my grandpa started to feel sick it was my sister and I, not your family, who took turns spending the night at their house to help out. How often I sat there in the living room when my grandmother was in a bad mood and decided to take it out on my poor grandfather! We all knew how badly she treated him. She was always screaming at him and telling him what to do. Grandpa was such a quiet man. I can still close my eyes and see him sitting in his rocking chair on the front porch, waving his hand and smiling at everyone who happened to walk by. In my opinion it was a blessing that he died when he did. He found the peace he deserved and he was finally able to get away from her.

Dad, we were so poor! There were times when all we had to eat was bread and coffee for breakfast and oatmeal for dinner. When we ran out of money and food we had to swallow our pride and go begging for money around the neighborhood. By the time I was 10 years old I had started working in the fields, planting vegetables and grains. My older siblings and I worked at our neighbor's coffee farm during the fall so that we could earn money and a bag of coffee. We gave my mother all the money to help with whatever was necessary around the house. Once the coffee season was over my siblings and I used to spend half the morning digging yams and potatoes from the ground so we could have dinner at the table. Even with all of us working, with no help from your family, we had to depend on neighbors and my mother's family to get through the month.

In our home everyone divided the house chores. The girls did the cleaning and cooking while the boys helped tend the few animals we had. We also walked though the woods collecting dry sticks for the fire pit so my mother could cook when we happened to run out of gas in the stove and didn't have the money to buy more. The summer seasons were extremely rough because of the drought. During those months the entire neighborhood was without running water for days or weeks at a time. Since water was not always available we had to help our mother by carrying our laundry to the nearby river so that she could wash our clothing. With the loads of laundry on our backs, we trudged down the road until we reached the river, often snaking through narrow passages in the mountains and along dried river beds until we reached the water. This was done every weekend. Most of that walking was done barefoot because we couldn't afford to damage the only pair of shoes we had. The women would spend most of the day doing the laundry and waiting for the clothes to dry on the rocks while my brothers and I spent the day resting up for the even more demanding uphill return.

By the time we got home we were sore, tired and hungry. The next morning we had to get up early.

Before leaving for school we carried barrels of water from a nearby spring on a generous neighbor's land so that my mother could cook and do dishes. Dad, I can't tell you how many times I lay in bed at night thinking about you and what my life could have been, or crying about what your absence had done to our lives.

Still, I cannot tell you how much I missed
you even though we never really met.
Growing up I wondered why mom never spoke
to us about you. I wanted to know about
your childhood, your first year in the
military and the first time you both met.
I wanted to learn about your likes and
dislikes, your character. As the saying
goes, be careful what you wish for.

You do recall that our neighbor was your
best friend and because of that he allowed
you to build our home on his property,
right next to his home? He became the
closest person we had to a father figure.
He was an exceptional man. He and his
family were better to us than your own
family was. He worked at a shoe factory
and from time to time he would come home
with shoes for us. These were our only
shoes, so we had to use them sparingly,
and often only for special occasions. I
grew up playing with his daughters, six of
them. There was also one boy who was much
older than we were so we didn't interact
much. To this day our family considers
them as family.

Our neighbor's wife was raising pigs and goats down the road from our house. Some days, after feeding the animals, she would stop over our house. The women sat outside on the porch, sipping coffee, talking about the good old days and watching the warm summer evenings disappear into the horizon, while the kids gathered in the yard to play all sorts of games. It was a blessing to have such wonderful neighbors.

I can't truthfully say that we were the perfect kids. Many times we did things that got us in trouble. While the women were sitting there talking, my sister and I would hide behind the house smoking the leftover cigarette butts we collected after my neighbor's husband discarded them. We got so high from the smoke! I suspect our mother knew about it but didn't reprimand us. I think she had far more important things to worry about and felt that we worked so hard that she didn't want to deprive us of such fleeting pleasures. One time my younger brother threw a rock at another brother and cut a gash in his head. Luckily we were able to get medical attention for him since free care was available for such a serious injury. I don't remember how many stitches he needed, but it was bad.

We tried very hard to fit in with the rest of the kids in the neighborhood. Mom did a good job raising us and trying to make our life as normal as possible but it wasn't easy. Because of our bad economic situation, we walked the neighborhood barefoot. I remember one time when I was trying to help my sister build a playhouse - I believe I was around 12 years old - I didn't realize that there was a rusted nail in the ground and I stepped on it. This wasn't considered a serious enough problem to qualify for free care, so I just had to take my chances with tetanus. The mark is still on my right foot as proof. Unfortunately for us, the only pair of shoes we had was reserved for school and special occasions including the holiday season.

School was about fifteen to twenty minutes walk and it was all uphill. From first grade to sixth grade we walked the same path each morning carrying a load of books; One book for each class. Sometimes we carried 5 books at once. School buses were only available for students from seventh grade to high school because their school was far away from the village. I enjoyed going to school not because I enjoy learning but because each school in Puerto Rico provided the best lunches for free. The school cafeteria served pasta or rice, vegetables, bread, milk and juice. If I knew my mother was running out of food at home, I tried to eat as much as possible because I knew that was going to be the only good meal of the day. School days were so long. We arrived in school for 7:30 am and we stayed until around 3:30 pm. We walk back home, change our outfits and start doing our shores. Only after everything was doing, my mother let us go play with the neighborhood kids. I recall one particular school function, one of my shoelaces broke and I had to run to the neighbor's and ask to borrow one from the girls. To my embarrassment I was left with two shoelaces that did not match at all. The year I entered sixth grade was very special to every student in our school. Sixth grade was the last year in primary school, you get to graduate with a ceremony and a party and most important, I knew I didn't have to walk to school again. I was excited about holding a diploma and being part of the graduation ceremony. Dad, Thanks to you, my mother couldn't pay the fee required and she couldn't come up with the money for the outfit we all had to buy for the ceremony. Instead, I had the school principal send the certificate with another student. Although I was upset, I kept telling myself that everything was going to be alright; that everything was going to change for the best. Little did I know, things were about to get worse in our life.

Most of the children in our neighborhood spent the summers playing sports, swimming and enjoying their childhood. We had to work. In the free times we had, we rested. I enjoyed spending time alone, gazing at the sky. It was freedom for me, freedom from everything. Under those clear skies I would lie down in the grass on a warm summer night and stare at the stars and the moon, wondering if there were other people living somewhere in the universe. I would look for figures made by the clouds. My favorite spot was in front of your mother's house. There was a cliff, right below which was the main road, but when you looked up, at the top of this huge mountain, was where our other grandparents lived. They were the complete opposite of your mother.

My mother's parents were a mixed race couple. My grandmother was about 4'2 with long straight hair, pale-skinned with blue eyes. She was sweeter than a peach. She was always delighted when we came to her house and would take us out back to teach us how to milk the goats and cows. It was always an adventure with her. Grandma had this habit of smoking a cigar every night and I loved sitting next to her, embraced by the aroma of tobacco. My grandpa was about 5'11 skinny, dark-skinned with curly hair. He was more reserved and, to tell you the truth, until the day he died I was a little afraid of him. He presented a tough facade and both the grandchildren and his own children respected him a great deal. I know that deep inside of him there was a soft side. He would make the journey from the mountains on weekends to bring us something, even if it was just milk and bread. He died while I was here in the States and I never got the chance to tell him how much I loved him.

There in my favorite place in the little free time I had, I dared to cry so many tears. That was the one place I could spend time alone, free from our daily responsibilities, and dream about my future and my goals: a future that I hoped bitterly would be far from there.

When I think about the things I went through, I cannot help but wonder if those memories were just a figment of my imagination or a bad dream. My life is so different now! But I know that they are as real as the tears rolling down my cheeks.

The holiday season was especially rough for us. We never had a real Christmas tree like everyone else in the neighborhood. We made ours from dried tree branches and took aluminum foil and color paper to make them into bulbs. When we were teenagers we saved enough money and bought real lights. A funny story happened one Christmas season when my brother and I were still too young to know the dangers of electricity. We waited until my mother was outside and we decided to see what I would look like with Christmas lights wrapped around my entire body. My mother almost had a heart attack when she walked into the living room and saw me wrapped in the lights. I'll never forget how fast my brother ran out of the house and left me plugged into the wall. It sounds funny right now but was no laughing matter when my mother grabbed the leather belt. We never did get close to that tree again.

Back in those days it was a custom for all parents to dress their children with new outfits for Christmas. I can't remember how many Christmas seasons we ended up wearing old outfits because our mother didn't have the money to buy us new ones. She had two choices: buy us outfits or spend the little money she had on food. Although we knew how hard it was for Mom to keep the home running and that it was more important to have food on the table every night, it was nevertheless a cause of shame for us kids to be the only ones in tattered clothes at Christmas.

My mother somehow always managed to buy us toys, even if only one. There was always something under the bed on January 6, the Three Magic Kings' day as we call it back home. Still, we resented getting so little. We worked so hard all year while other kids played, we got so little pleasure out of our childhood, we felt that we deserved more. Instead we had nothing! Looking back now, I view things differently. We may have received little but we had everything because we had each other. That realization has enhanced the meaning of holidays for me. My mother worked hard to get us where we are today. I wish I could repay her a million times over for everything she did for us.

Our house had only a small living room, two long narrow bedrooms, one on each side of the family room, a dining room and a small kitchen. I still marvel at how so many people managed to live in such a small place. In one of the bedrooms, two of my brothers shared one bed and my younger brother and I shared the other. In the other bedroom, my two sisters shared one bed and my mother had her own. My mother's bed was a high four-poster bed on which she always had a pretty bedspread. The living room was extremely small. Whenever we had company the kids had to stay outside or in the bedrooms because there was no room for anyone to walk through.

We had the same television for around 15 years. It was a black and white model with tubes inside that occasionally would burn out so mom had to call someone to come and replace them. By the time I was 10 years old our house had started to show its age thanks to years of extreme summer heat, old paint that was peeling, and damage from termites. The floors were down to bare plywood. It had been covered by linoleum but all that was left were pieces here and there. There were holes in the living room floor, the biggest right when you walked into the front door. You could see under the house. Oh dad, as I tell you these things I wonder how my mother found the strength to make it through those years. Her faith in God and love for her children must have given her the strength she needed to go on.

It was not until our oldest brother was old enough to learn to use tools that we were able to start fixing the house. In fact dad, because of him, we ended up rebuilding our home. He had gone to Pennsylvania to work at my uncle's mushroom farm and had saved enough money to buy materials to fix the house. His absence was extremely hard for everyone. We were such a close family. Back then we didn't have computers or telephones in our home so we had to rely on letters sent back and forth. My mom hated it when he left but she knew we had no choice. When he came home from the States, everyone in the neighborhood gathered at the house and helped pour concrete for our new floor. My brother changed the entire layout of the house. We started to let go of the past and your legacy. By the time I left the country nothing in that house reminded me of you, except of course the picture on the wall. When I look at that picture, the only picture we have of you, I am amazed to see our resemblance. I look just like you did in your early twenties. I often found myself wondering if it would be worth learning anything about you…

"When I'm old enough to make my own decisions and make enough money to buy a plane ticket, I'm going to move to the States. I'm going to have everything I always wanted: I'll be rich and famous and am going to speak English just like my neighbor's kids do. And I'll never be poor again." That's what I told friends back then. You have no idea how much I hated our impoverished conditions. I used to sit alone near our grandmother's house daydreaming about what my life would have been like had I been born somewhere else. I wondered what it would be like to have everything, to be able to buy toys, go to private school, and go on vacations to foreign lands. For us, Walt Disney World was a magical place that only existed on television.

I didn't want to die and be buried on the same ground where you are resting, father. After what you had done, I wanted to be nothing like you, and as far from your memory as I could be.

We went to public schools because it was free and convenient.

Everyone was required to wear the same uniform to promote equality in the school. Unfortunately some kids came to school with brand new shoes and designer accessories. We didn't have that luxury and wore whatever was on sale at the store. Some kids were understanding but most were cruel. Some kids also made fun of me because I was small. I had such a complex, dad! I felt ugly. I couldn't understand why I was skinny and short. Kids would walk by me in the halls and push me to the side. I would run to the bathroom and sit there and cry, and wish I had a dad like everyone else to defend me. But you were gone and I was alone.

To make matters worse, I was facing a major problem in school. I couldn't memorize things or pay attention to the teachers. I had to study harder than the other students in my class did. I studied for exams for days, only to forget most of it once I was in the classroom. Not only did I feel ugly, I also felt stupid. It wasn't until I was in my mid twenties that a specialist diagnosed me with what is called Processing disorder. This is a condition where the brain can't process fast enough. Too many people talking at the same time is like a beehive to my brain. When the doctor found out about this, he couldn't believe that I'd been able to graduate from high school, go to college for three years and, even more impressive, had been able to learn a second language within a year of arriving in the States. I suppose that my desire to succeed was stronger than my limitations.

The three years I spent in college were extremely hard for me. After graduating from high school, I decided to follow in my sister's footsteps and get a higher education. In spite of having little money to send two of us to college, Mama decided that it would be in my best interests to get an education.

The first two years of tuition were paid for with financial aid but that is about all I had received. The books were my responsibility and were very expensive, especially for someone with no money. I arranged my schedule so that my first class started at 8:30 A.M. That gave me time to get up at 5:00 A.M., shower, dress and have breakfast. After I was done, I walked down to the main road and hitchhiked to campus. There were few times when I was lucky enough to get a ride all the way to school. Other times I took a ride to the center of town and from there I waited for another ride to college. I had to do this almost everyday because I rarely had money to pay the bus fare. The entire trip from my house to college was about two hours, including the waiting. I can't tell you how many times I stood by the road waiting for a ride only to turn around because it was too late to go to school. There were times when I found a ride to town and then waited for hours to get a ride to college. Occasionally I ended up having to walk from the center of town back to the village where I lived. It took me about two hours to walk home. By the time I got home, my eyes were swollen from my tears of frustration.

Most of the time I did manage to get to school. There were times when I got home from college with a headache or stomachache from not eating all day. I had no money to buy lunch so I would spend the day hungry: instead of buying lunch I saved all my money for books. My mother helped me out the best that she could under the circumstances, with the little money she received from social security and by borrowing money from neighbors. It was just too much for her. Mama felt so powerless and guilty. But it was not her fault, dad: it was yours.

My circle of friends in college was the same circle of friends I had had back in high school. At the end of our senior year we had decided that we wanted to stay together so we had signed up for the same classes. The few times they found out that I didn't eat for lack of money, they invited me to eat and paid for my lunch. I didn't like depending on anyone for food. I was stubborn. I thought that since I had survived my childhood years, I could face any hardship on my own. After just a few such lunches, I had started to feel badly enough about having my friends buy lunch for me that I began making excuses. Some days I told them that I was sick to my stomach and could not eat. Other times I said that I was going to meet someone for lunch in town. While everyone was having lunch at the cafeteria, I went to the library to study for my upcoming exams and tried to ignore my hunger.

In the spring of 1985, I was forced to drop out of school. I received a letter from financial aid stating that my benefits had been cut in half. I was devastated. I had wanted to succeed so badly that I had compromised my health - I was 20 years old and my weight had dropped to a dangerously low 105 lbs. - and still it wasn't enough. Money, the one thing we had always lacked, showed itself once again to be of utmost importance.

Dear father, it has been extremely hard for me to write this letter without shedding some tears. A few times I had to stop writing because the tears blurred the screen. I want you to know how painful it is to remember my past. My college years in particular were the worst for me because I had pinned my hopes on a good education to help our family get out of the situation you got us into. No child should have to fight that hard to get an education. No family should have to fight that hard to survive.

I didn't know how to break the news to my

friends because I had too much pride. I kept quiet until I could figure out an excuse for dropping out of school: perhaps that I wanted to get a job or that

I was bored with classes. I was not sure what to say. I was too hurt to think at all. Summer was around the corner and I planned to use the time to think.

It was a beautiful spring day and I was doing some chores around the house. I remember waking up that day full of energy. I'm not sure why, but I felt as if something wonderful was about to happen. I saw my mother coming down the stairs to the basement, where I was cutting wood. She had a smile on her face. I stopped what I was doing and sat to rest for a minute.

"Your uncle is coming home from the States to visit for few weeks," my mom announced.

"That's great news. Do you have any idea if our cousins are coming as well?"

"Yes, the entire family is supposed to be here next week and they will be staying with your grandmother Estella."

Destiny has a way of knocking at the door when you least expect it. We knew that my uncle was coming to visit us from the States. What we were not prepared for was the invitation he extended to my brother and me to go live with him and his family in the States.

I was a little apprehensive. I'd never been away from my family. My uncle strove to convince me. He said that this trip was going to be fun and that my brother and I needed a change of scenery. We heard about all the job opportunities waiting for us. Everything I had always dreamed seemed to be just around the corner.

At first my mother refused to give me permission to go. I think she was concerned about breaking up a family that had been so close for so many years. My uncle convinced her by emphasizing that it would be in the family's best interests if we were able to help out financially.

Our next step was to try to figure out how

to get money to pay for our airplane tickets. Our uncle offered to pay for them but we could not accept.

"Uncle, you've done more than enough by letting us go to live with you and offering to help us find jobs, we can't let you pay for our tickets too," I said to him.

By then I'd forgotten about the part-time work study job I'd had at the college library during my last semester. It had just been for a few days a week, a few hours a day. My job was to check in and file returned books, work on the filing cabinets, and help other students find the books they were looking for. I loved my job. I felt important, perhaps because someone always needed me. The librarian was pleased with my organizational skills and the fact that I took my job seriously. One day while filing together, she mentioned to me how happy she was that I was working that semester because most of the students who had held that job in the past were only there for the money and didn't seem to care about showing up on time or doing the job right. The library had been my first paying job. The first two years of college I had qualified for financial assistance that helped to pay for tuition, but in my third year my grant had been reduced so I had applied for a work study job. I was happy to be productive and to be able to help pay for my education but I did have one complaint: the pay came only at the end of the semester.

But destiny had been at work even in the apparent setback of the reduction in my financial aid and in the delayed payment for my work study job. It just so happened that the check came as we were trying to figure out where we would get money for the tickets to the States. My mother had agreed to let us go and, before she could change her mind, we went to town and bought non-refundable tickets.

As the saying goes "April showers bring May flowers." Unfortunately for us, that year, 1985, the rain extended beyond

April, through the first few weeks of May. During the weeks prior to our trip it rained constantly. The forecast called for rain through the following week - the week of our trip. I thought for sure that the flight was going to be cancelled due to weather. I prayed as I'd never prayed before, glued to the TV, hoping for a change in the forecast. It didn't occur to me that a cancelled flight is usually just delayed, so we would still be able to go. I had so much hope invested in the trip that it was hard for me to wait for the planned departure date, let alone have to wait for even one more day. Happily the rain did give way before the departure date arrived.

Dear father, I want to clarify something with you: in spite of the excitement about the trip, I spent that entire week thinking about my family. At one point I locked myself in the basement so that nobody could hear me cry. I was so sad to leave behind the ones I cared about the most, the ones who, like me, had fought to survive the grinding poverty you had left behind. I was tormented at the thought of abandoning them as you had done to us. I was tormented with worries about their fate.

May 11, 1985. I will never forget that day. It was only 4:00 A.M. and I was already up and looking out the window toward the horizon, anxiously waiting for the sun to come out. I had not been able to sleep at all that night, my mind consumed by thoughts of the trip and of my family.

My mother got up and came to see if I was ok. At the sound of her voice, my eyes filled with tears and I started to choke up and couldn't speak a word. She understood my pain so she went back to bed and left me sitting in the dark just before dawn, staring at the clock and willing its hands to move faster. Everyone was sound asleep and I just paced back and forth from the living room to the porch watching for the time to pass and the sun to come up. Around 6:30 I showered and dressed. By 8:00 my family was up and doing chores. Nobody was talking. It was as if someone had died and the air was filled with sadness. I knew that when the time came I wasn't going to be able to say goodbye to anyone so I just walked out the back door when nobody was watching and waited for the car down the road. I got in the back seat with my brother and we drove away. Not once did I dare to look back. I couldn't. My destiny seemed just a flight away, and I was afraid that if I looked back, my heart wouldn't let me get on that flight.

When I arrived in the States, a sense of peace came over me. It was as if something had been waiting for me for so long. I cried for the ones I'd left behind and their uncertain future. I had come here to help them but I knew in my heart that I was going to stay forever. I found peace knowing that the rest of my family would follow one day, and they did.

To this day I'm haunted by the painful memories of my past, the struggles you put us through. I cry when I think about all that I have now that we had wished we'd had then. I want to feel at home in the States, to feel free, safe, and at peace. But my past and I hold each other in a poisonous embrace. I finally realized that I have to let go and, for the first time, I'm not afraid to speak about my life.

In spite of everything that happened to us I can't say that everything was bad. I learned so much. I learned to value my family, to value what I have. I learned that sometimes you need to let go of your pride in order to allow others to help you. I think the most important lesson of all was to trust in God and believe that dreams do come true. I'm not sure if I could go back and relive my life but I welcome the lessons it taught me. I'll die knowing that we did the best we could within our power to survive.

It's already the beginning of autumn here in New England and the night arrives ever earlier. The foliage is the most amazing transformation I have ever seen during a change of seasons. The cold air of winter fills the early hours of the morning. My nightmares are outdated and I'm happy with my life. I know where I came from, who I am and where I want to be. I'm at a point of my life where all the pieces are starting to come together and the puzzle is just about finished. To help complete it, I needed to tell the world about this painful part of my life.

Although I'll never forget what happened to us because of you, I decided that the time to move on is now. My dreams are coming true. I've found the place I always dreamt I wanted to be, the place where I should've been from the very start: home. That place is right here… right now.

My life doesn't stop here but hopefully my shame and resentment do. Hopefully I have learned from your mistakes and can be the man you weren't. I lost my pride as a child but I gained love and respect in the world because of my story.

Sincerely,

Antonio

As I grew older, I had fewer dreams and more courage and eventually, those childhood dreams became reality. At the same time, those dreams which I used to enjoy so much became nightmares. Now as an adult, I'm afraid to dream."

CHAPTER V

The message

"Can I ask you a question, dad?" Fernando asked.

"Of course you can Fernando."

"When did you lose your childhood and become a man?"

"Well son, that question is not so simple. To start, I am still a child at heart. There are many times in my life I could say I became a man. I became a man when I came to the realization that my family needed an extra set of hands to help with whatever was necessary around the house. I became a man again when I struck out on my own, coming to the United States to work for a better life for me and my family. Or maybe it was the day I married your mother, or the day I found the courage to confront my hidden childhood. Or maybe it was the day we adopted you, son. Becoming a man is not something that is defined by one event... It seems that God always provides us with defining moments in our lives."

"Do you have any regrets?"

"I did. I spent most of my life being angry at God, asking Him 'Why me, why us?' There were many times when I looked up to Heaven and asked Him, why did you give us such a rough road to walk when others had a paved road? I couldn't understand why the Bible says that He loves His children and yet we were suffering and He did not lift His hand to help us at all. Little did I know God had been holding us in His arms each and every step of the way.

"Life works in mysterious ways and it was not until recent years that I found the answer," I continued." We did to survive we did as a team. Someone's failure was everyone's failure. Nobody was jealous of the other's achievement because when one of us succeeded, it meant more bread on the table for all of us. God knew exactly what He was doing when He picked my family for this journey. Suddenly, the answer to that question became as clear as a fine summer day and once again, He proved to me that He was always right. When I asked 'Lord, Why us?' His answer was 'Because I knew your family could handle it, when so many others could not.'

"I want you to remember this one thing: 'God helps those who help themselves.' Each of us has a purpose: painters can inspire people through the power of their vision, poets with the beauty of their words and musicians with the ability to portray emotion through sound. But you decide your future through your actions, not by sitting around waiting for miracles to happen. My life has changed because I believed and because I dreamt but above all because I persevered."

Fernando turned toward me and said sheepishly, "I hope you're not upset by the fact that I brought this subject up, especially now, under these circumstances. I felt that it was very important for me to know. I owe it to Grandma to learn all I can about her before she dies."

"Fernando, you need to understand that the right time for the story to be told was whenever you felt ready to hear it. You had the right to know and you did me a favor by asking. You were the last person

I was afraid to tell. Your bravery in bringing this up and your understanding may finally free me of my nightmares. You mean the world to me and I promise never to keep a secret from you again."

"Death can take away the physical part of those we love the most but there's few things death can't take away; the memories, the love and promise that one day we will be reunited again".

CHAPTER VI

The last breath

Shortly after I finished telling my story my sister came outside and with tears in her eyes said somberly, "Antonio, Fernando, you both need to come in now. I believe the time has come."

Fernando hurried back inside and she followed him. I stood there on the porch, my entire body frozen in place. I felt like I could not move, or perhaps I wanted time to stand still so as to prevent my mother's passing.

"I can't face this right now, I can't let go of her, not yet," I protested. But I forced myself to take slow steps until I reached the room. Laura reached for my hand and pulled me close to her. I stared at Mama, holding back my tears. There she is, as beautiful as I remember her being when I was a child. Her long hair pulled into a ponytail. The candlelight was casting a soft glow on her face and eyes. She lifted her hand as if reaching for a door or a light.

The rest of my siblings, nieces and

nephews gathered around the bed. To our collective astonishment, my brother started to speak:

"Mama, we love you so much. You gave us unconditional love. We will never forget you."

My sister followed my brother. "You have given us the greatest gifts of all: unity and love, and for that we bless you."

Without thinking about it, I walked to the bed and taking Mama's hand in mine, I started to speak: "Mama, you have done so much for us. You taught us to love one another, to work hard for what we want; to value everything that life brings our way, no matter how good or bad. You taught us never to take things for granted. You once said that everything happens for a reason, and today we are a testament to your belief. Mama, you fought hard and you won the battle. The time has come for you to let go of everything. Start your journey and find the peace that for so long you have been searching for. The light of God is here to help guide you to a better place. Know that someday we will be reunited and when that time comes, everything is going to be wonderful."

Mama opened her eyes and spoke with surprising strength:

"We did have a great dance, my son, we really did."

She looked around at each of us.

She smiled and took a deep breath, her last breath. She closed her eyes to the world and sighed contentedly, feeling peace and happiness because she knew she was finally going home.

The day of the funeral everyone gathered in church for a mass. We decided to dress in white instead of black because we felt that black was for mourning and on this day we were about to celebrate my mother's life and her achievements. White symbolizes peace, my mother loved white doves and as a kid I recall watching her feed the ones around the house. When the casket was about to be lay down in the ground, each member of the family release a dove as a sign of peace and gratitude. After the funeral procession the family went back to her home. Food was already delivered by a catering Co. We sat around the living. We spoke about the ceremony and the amount of people who came to the funeral. This was the first time since all of us were gathered around without my mother. We started recounting memories from our past, the way we used to fight and play and the things that happened during the holidays. My little brother Estevan who's been extremely shy his entire life stood up and walked toward the bedroom door. He was leaning again the door frame with his hand in his pockets and tears streaming down his cheeks.

"What's going to happen now? Where do we go from here? She was our foundation; I came to her for everything. I feel so lost without her."

I walked toward him and place one hand over his shoulder. Javier turned around and started to cry in my shoulder. "Little brother, I know how attached you were to mom, but just remember, we are all here for you. Our mother is still here in spirit and I know she is going to guide us through life. She won't do what our father did to us"

My sister Delia also stood up and asked everyone to hold hands. Once the chain was form, she continued to speak.

"Our mother suffered a great length when we were kids to make sure we stay together as a family. Now that she is gone, we need to keep her legacy alive. We have to promise that not matter what, we will stay in touch and we are going to continue celebrating holidays the same way she thought us."

CHAPTER VII

The legacy

Ten years have passed since our mother crossed into the light and a better life. The place she had called home for 20 years sat empty until my brother Felipe got married and decided to move in with his wife and two children. When mom passed away we had all agreed that every five years we were going to have a reunion to celebrate her life. The time has come and today everyone has gathered at the same house. It's amazing to see how my nieces and nephews have grown! Some are already married with family of their own. When Laura and I walk in, everyone is talking and laughing. The voices of children playing in the yard can be heard.

Felipe has also maintained our mother's garden in her honor. We all help to preserve the garden when we can. Our mother invested so much of herself into it that we couldn't bear to see it overrun. She often referred to the flowers as her green babies. The garden stands as a tribute to our mother's excellent parenting.

"Hello father, hello mother. I'm so happy to see you again," Fernando yells from the far corner of the room, pushing through the crowd to greet us.

Fernando is 25 years old now and is working as an architect in Phoenix. Five months ago he married his high school sweetheart, Stephanie, and shortly afterwards they relocated to Phoenix, where Fernando had received a good job offer from a reputable firm.

"Hi son, how's married life treating you? And where's

Stephanie? I hope you brought her with you."

"She's here, in the ki..." he begins, stopping as Stephanie comes out of the kitchen, running into our arms, and giving each of us a hug and a kiss.

"And we have great news for both of you. You're going to be grandparents! We found out last month that we're pregnant!" Stephanie beams.

"What do you mean last month?! Stephanie, Antonio and I are a little hurt that you waited so long to tell us about the baby," Laura sighs theatrically, obviously joking.

Stephanie places her hand on her chest and makes a comically sad face. "I'm sorry, it was my entire fault. Please don't blame Fernando. I wanted to tell you in person."

"Oh Lord, you know I'm still too young to be called Grandma," Laura laughs. "I'm so happy for both of you! I cannot wait to baby-sit my…" she trails off, expectantly, fishing for information about the sex of the baby.

"Do you know whether it's a boy or a girl?" I ask, excitedly following Laura's lead.

"It's going to be a girl, dad,"

Stephanie replies.

Excited, Fernando moved in the middle of the room and called for everyone's attention.

"Everyone, please listen. Stephanie and I discussed it and decided that our baby would be named Helen, after our grandmother. A woman as exceptional as she was deserves to have her name attached to our first-born."

The house falls into silence for a moment. Everyone looks from Fernando to Stephanie and then the room erupts with enthusiastic approval of this announcement.

"Fernando, your grandmother would be so proud of you," Laura says, hugging Fernando.

"Not to mention how happy she would be to have the baby named after her," my sister Delia adds.

Fernando pleased but a little self-conscious because of the family's reactions, replies, "Our grandmother should be remembered for her courage and her loving nature. Although I'm not a blood relative she always made sure to show how much she loved me and how happy she was that I was part of this family.

"Auntie Delia, the day grandma died, my father told me the story of your childhood. It must have been horrible growing up in those circumstances. I have so much respect for every one of you and

I'm very proud to belong to this family," he concludes.

My sister smiled widely and gave Fernando a fierce hug and a kiss. She turned and walked away then she stopped halfway across the room, turned back to us and called to Fernando. He looked up at her. She smiled and said loudly, making sure that everyone can hear: "No, Fernando, we're the ones proud that you are part of our family."

When I heard my sister say that to my son, I started to cry. A refreshing breeze whispers through the open windows, carrying the scent of roses from the garden as if our mother, watching us from heaven, was blessing that moment.

It is clear that her legacy of love was still alive.

Our children will have a better future because of the struggles we faced in our past and because of our love and unity as a family gave us the strength to continue our journey through life. It feels good to be home everyone, it really does...

"Life is about taking chances and following your dreams. Those who dare to dream and risk it all for the sake of their future will someday collect the fruit of their efforts"

ABOUT THE BOOK

I didn't want to finish my book without first giving you some facts and thoughts. The story and characters in the book was a product of my imagination, the part of the Letter is based on real facts and events that helped shaped the man I am today. Of course, I did use fictitious names to protect people's privacy.

Although life as a child was rough by all standards, I did have many good memories that will be treasured for ever. I remember running and playing in the prairies, going for a swim at the nearby river; I remember sitting by the porch under the clear blue skies waiting for clouds to form into sculptures and lying down in the grass at night watching for a shooting star to pass across the heavens. It might not seem a lot to some people but for an 8 year boy who had nothing but dreams, it was plenty.

Something most people will be surprise to hear about me is the fact that as a child I was extremely shy. It wasn't until the age of twenty that I started to come out of the shell. I have a condition called processing disorder but I was not diagnosed until I was in my mid 30's. That explains why during my school years I had a hard time trying to memorize for school exams. Other fact that most people don't know is that when I first came to Massachusetts, I came for a two weeks vacation and there was not way in hell anyone was going to make me return home. We drove away from the airport and took the mass pike toward the city of Worcester.

As we arrived into the area, I had a weird sensation that somehow, I've been there before. Everything looked familiar. Even the homes which are constructed different from the ones back home seemed familiar. I used to tell people that I was here in a previous life.

My family didn't know about this book until its publication. I wanted to keep it a secret for as long as I could because truthfully, I didn't know how they were going to react with me writing our story.

It's already 2009. Our mother is over 72 yrs. She continues to travel to Puerto Rico twice a year to visit her mother who's about 97 yrs. When I look at my mother I see the same woman I used to remember back in the days when we were children but deep inside I know that she's getting older and I wonder how long will she keep going. I'm afraid to find out what's going to happen once my grandmother dies because I believe my mother's strength come from knowing that even from a far, my grandma still depends on her. I guess life is a cycle and that too should come to and end as it is for each one of us.

ABOUT THE AUTHOR

Alberto Mercado was born in Puerto Rico to a family of modest means. A subsequent family tragedy left the family fatherless and struggling to get by. With no outside help forthcoming, the family pulled together, with each member playing his or her own role in daily life in an effort to survive. But their hardships, in contrast to many of the families around them, instilled a desire to succeed. Alberto strove valiantly to improve his lot, initially frustrated by financial hardships and other factors. He had long dreamed of escaping to the United States, the Land of Opportunity. Given the chance to realize this dream, he has never looked back.

Alberto has established a long career in medical service. He has recently explored a love of photography, a pursuit which has brought him some press coverage and several exhibitions. In writing a brief self-introduction for one of his exhibitions, the seeds of his first book, the book that you are reading right now, were planted. His brief biography generated strong emotional responses from some readers who encouraged him to more fully tell his story. The end result is not a biography but is inspired by many actual events in Alberto's life.

These childhood years forged in Alberto a man who appreciates family and friendships. He remains very close with his family and, as a friend of his, I can attest that Alberto has established and tries to maintain annual traditions that reunite his friends - even when it seems that everyone is caught up in their own individual world. I and his other friends appreciate this effort.

The events in this book may or may not resemble those of your own life but I'm sure that you can find within its pages something of value, and hopefully it brings you a newfound appreciation for that intimate circle of family and friends that makes your life as rich as it is.

3297750

Made in the USA